DISCARD

FIREFIGHTERS to the RESCUE!

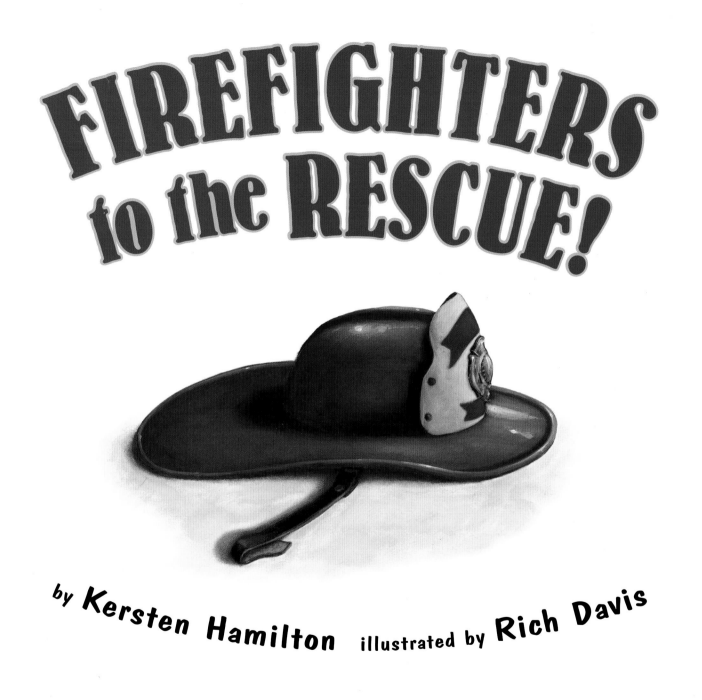

by **Kersten Hamilton**   illustrated by **Rich Davis**

VIKING

VIKING

Published by Penguin Group
Penguin Young Readers Group, 345 Hudson Street, New York, New York 10014, U.S.A.
Penguin Group (Canada), 10 Alcorn Avenue, Toronto, Ontario, Canada M4V 3B2
(a division of Pearson Penguin Canada Inc.)
Penguin Books Ltd, 80 Strand, London WC2R 0RL, England
Penguin Ireland, 25 St Stephen's Green, Dublin 2, Ireland (a division of Penguin Books Ltd)
Penguin Group (Australia), 250 Camberwell Road, Camberwell, Victoria 3124, Australia
(a division of Pearson Australia Group Pty Ltd)
Penguin Books India Pvt Ltd, 11 Community Centre, Panchsheel Park, New Delhi — 110 017, India
Penguin Group (NZ), Cnr Airborne and Rosedale Roads, Albany, Auckland, New Zealand
(a division of Pearson New Zealand Ltd)
Penguin Books (South Africa) (Pty) Ltd, 24 Sturdee Avenue, Rosebank, Johannesburg 2196, South Africa

Penguin Books Ltd, Registered Offices: 80 Strand, London WC2R 0RL, England

First published in 2005 by Viking, a division of Penguin Young Readers Group

10 9 8 7 6 5 4 3 2

Text copyright © Kersten Hamilton, 2005
Illustrations copyright © Rich Davis, 2005
All rights reserved

Library of Congress Cataloging-in-Publication Data is available.
ISBN 0-670-03503-3

Book design by Jim Hoover

Manufactured in China
Set in Don Casual Extended

For Mark, who has always been the
wind beneath my wings.——K. H.

To Dad, who continues to show me in a million
little ways, "you can do about anything if you stay
with it long enough." I love you!——Rich

Firefighters
working hard.
Cooking,
mopping,
making beds.

Playing tricks
on sleepyheads.

Suddenly—

On go boots
and coats and hats.
Ready? Right!
All aboard and
hold on tight!

Out the doors into the street.

FIREFIGHTERS
TO THE RESCUE!

Horn blowing, engine roaring.
Red lights, blue lights
flash a warning.
Move aside—
fire truck coming!

Passing busses,
bikes and cabs,
zooming fast
down the hill

past cars at
stoplights
standing still.

An orange glow.
I see the fire!
FIREFIGHTERS TO THE RESCUE!

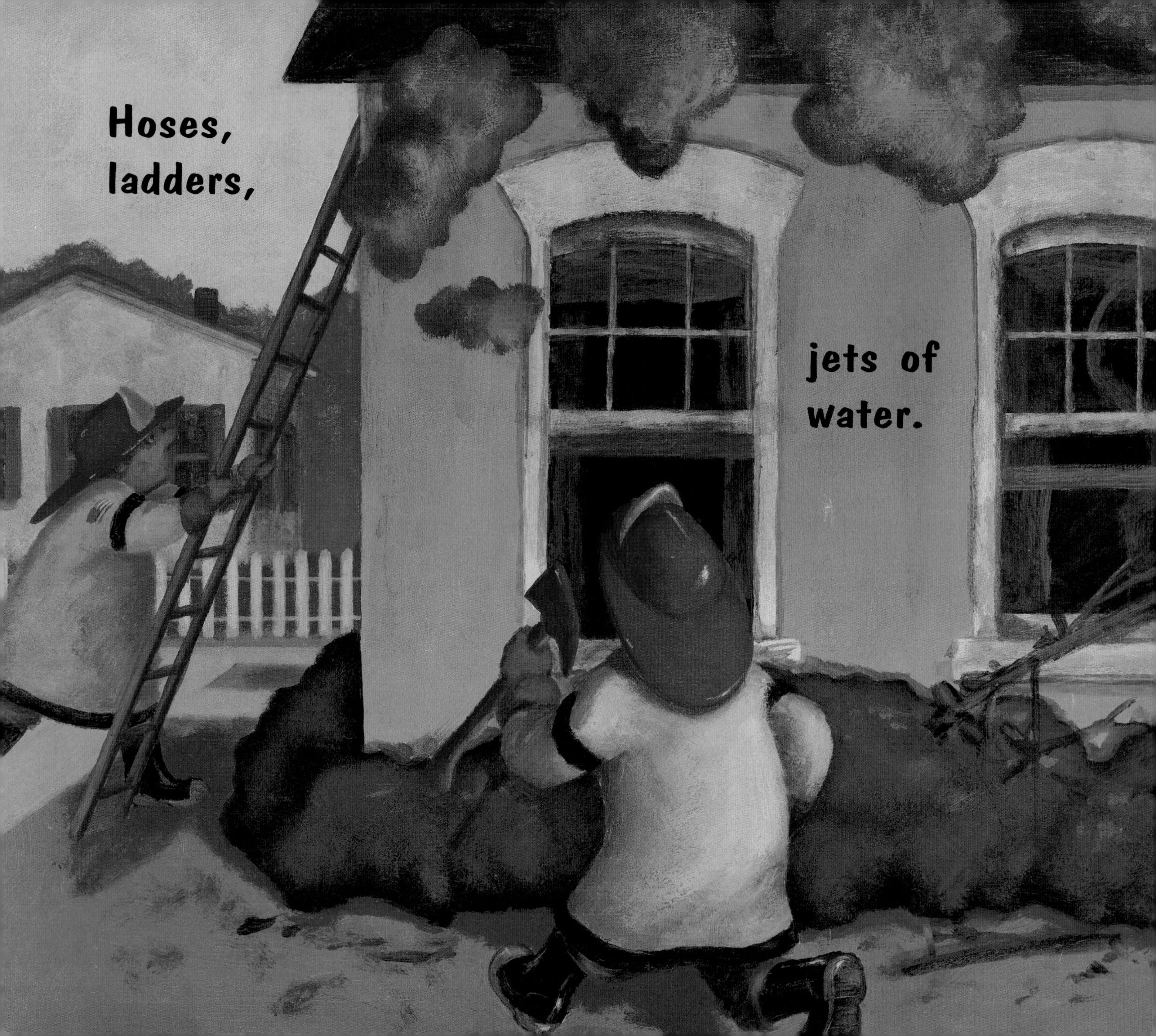

Hoses,
ladders,

jets of
water.

Someone calling,
"Where's my Ben?
I can't find him!"

Firefighters
going in!

People
watch and
wait and pray
and then

Through the dark,
through the smoke,
a bright red hat,
a yellow coat.

Hear them yell!
Hear them shout!

FIREFIGHTERS TO THE RESCUE!